nickelodeon

SpongeBob SQUAREPANTS

Batter Up, SpongeBob!

by David Lewman
illustrated by Warner McGee

Simon Spotlight/Nickelodeon
New York   London   Toronto   Sydney

Stephen Hillenburg

Based on the TV series *SpongeBob SquarePants*™ created by Stephen Hillenburg as seen on Nickelodeon™

SIMON SPOTLIGHT / NICKELODEON
New York London Toronto Sydney
1230 Avenue of the Americas, New York, New York 10020
© 2011 Viacom International Inc. All rights reserved. NICKELODEON. *SpongeBob SquarePants*, and all related
titles, logos, and characters are trademarks of Viacom International Inc. Created by Stephen Hillenburg.
All rights reserved, including the right of reproduction in whole or in part in any form.
SIMON SPOTLIGHT and colophon are registered trademarks of Simon & Schuster, Inc.
For information about special discounts for bulk purchases, please contact Simon & Schuster Special Sales at
1-866-506-1949 or business@simonandschuster.com.
Manufactured in the United States of America 0211 LAK
10 9 8 7 6 5 4 3 2
ISBN 978-1-4424-1379-5

"Sure, Dad, I'd love to play on your new baseball team!" SpongeBob said to his father.

He hung up his shell phone. "Gary, this is going to be so *great*! I used to play baseball when I was just a little sponge, and I loved it!"

"I was good, too. Slugger SquarePants, they called me!" SpongeBob said as he pretended to swing a bat.

"Meow?" asked Gary.

"Oh, sure," SpongeBob answered, nodding. "I still remember how to play. All I need is a little practice."

That gave SpongeBob an idea. "I'd better go down to the basement and dig out my equipment."

"Let's see . . . soccer, football, sand hockey . . . where's my baseball stuff?"

Tossing gear behind him, SpongeBob rummaged in every box. "Aha!" he cried. "Here we go!"

SpongeBob triumphantly pulled a big, squishy ball out of a trunk. He also found a tee to put the ball on, a fat plastic bat, and a glove. "Hey!" he cried, delighted. "My old cap!"

He placed the little cap onto his square head. "Still fits!" he exclaimed. Gary wasn't so sure.

SpongeBob carried all of his baseball equipment
to his front yard. He carefully balanced the squishy
ball on the tee. Just as he was about to swing his plastic
bat, he heard, "Hey, SpongeBob! What are you doing?"
    Startled, SpongeBob looked up to see Patrick and said,
"I'm just brushing up on my baseball skills!"

"Oh, boy!" Patrick shouted. "I *love* baseball!" Then he asked, "What's baseball?"

"Just watch and learn, pal," SpongeBob said. "The key is to keep your eye on the ball."

"It's easy to keep your eye on the ball when it doesn't go anywhere," Patrick said.

The next day SpongeBob went to the baseball field where his dad's team was playing. "Good thing I practiced. I want Dad to be proud of me!"

But when he got to the field he saw they weren't using squishy balls. They weren't using plastic bats. *They weren't even using tees!*

With his mouth hanging open, SpongeBob watched as the pitcher reared back and hurled a fastball. It came whizzing across the plate and smacked into the catcher's glove. *Whap!*

"Hey, SpongeBob!" yelled Patrick from the stands. "This is great!"

"You mean the fast pitching?" SpongeBob called back.

"No, the ice cream!" Patrick answered.

"Hi, Son!" called SpongeBob's dad cheerfully. "You made it just in time! The game is about to start and we're up at bat first."

"G-great!" SpongeBob said, trying to act calm.

His dad stepped up to the plate, swung, and got a hit!

"Go, Dad!" cheered SpongeBob as his dad ran. He was safe on first!

"Okay, Son," yelled SpongeBob's dad. "Your turn!"

SpongeBob didn't want to let his dad down. He'd have to give this scary version of baseball a try.

"Hey, SpongeBob!" Patrick shouted from the stands.

"Yeah, buddy?" asked SpongeBob, looking to his friend for encouragement.

"This ice-cold lemonade is refreshing too!"

SpongeBob walked over to the row of bats, trying to see which one was the smallest. He picked one up, and was amazed at how heavy it was.

"Batter up!" the umpire shouted impatiently.

SpongeBob nervously walked toward the plate, his knees shaking and his hands trembling.

"Hey, kid! Aren't you forgetting something?" yelled one of the other players with a snort. "You forgot your batting helmet."

He tossed SpongeBob a sturdy plastic helmet.

"Th-th-thanks," murmured SpongeBob as he took off his baseball cap and put on the hard helmet.

"Go, SpongeBob!" Patrick cheered. "Get a touchdown!"

SpongeBob stepped up to the plate. The catcher signaled the
pitcher, telling him what kind of pitch to throw. The pitcher nodded.
SpongeBob's knees were shaking. The pitcher looked to first base,
went into his windup, and *zizz!*—sent the ball rocketing across home plate.
SpongeBob never even got a chance to swing!
"*Strike one!*" called the umpire.

In no time at all the pitcher had thrown two more strikes. *"You're out!"* the umpire screamed.

"That's okay, SpongeBob!" his dad called from first base. "You'll get 'em next time!"

"Wonderful!" Patrick shouted. SpongeBob looked up at him, confused. "This popcorn is *wonderful!*" he explained.

SpongeBob felt better out on the field running after the ball. He was actually pretty good at throwing too.

But in no time at all it was his turn at bat again. He picked a bat, put on a batting helmet, and walked to the plate, trying to keep his knees from knocking.

He saw his dad watching from second base. SpongeBob took a deep breath, thinking, "Keep your eye on the ball!"

The pitcher pulled down his cap. He looked to the left. He looked to the right. Then he leaned way back and fired the ball toward home plate.

Keeping his eye on the ball, SpongeBob swung the bat and . . .

Dink! He got a hit! He couldn't believe it! He just stood there, staring at the ball rolling slowly through the grass.

"He shoots! He scores!" cheered Patrick from the stands.

"*Run, Spongebob, run!*" yelled his dad from second base.

"Oh, right!" SpongeBob said. He was so surprised he'd gotten a hit, he forgot to run!

SpongeBob ran as fast as he could to first base. The pitcher sprinted toward the ball, scooped it up, and tossed it to the first baseman . . .

But it went right past the first baseman! SpongeBob stepped on the base and yelled, "Dad, go!"

SpongeBob's dad rounded third and headed for home. The first baseman scrambled for the ball. He threw it to the catcher . . .

Just as SpongeBob's dad crossed the plate!

"Safe!" bellowed the umpire.

It was their team's first run! The crowd went wild!

"Goooaaaallll!" yelled Patrick.

SpongeBob and his dad's team went on to win the game!

HOME 0 0

VISITORS 0 0

"Nice game, slugger," SpongeBob's dad said to him as they walked off the field. "I'm proud of you!"

"Thanks, Dad!" SpongeBob said. "It was great playing with you again. Any time your team needs another player, I'm ready!"